Christmas Presence

Stories of the Christmas Miracles We Create

Jim Timonere

Someone you know needs the gift of your presence.
Share that gift as if every day were Christmas.
-Jim Timonere

Dedication

Twenty-seven years ago, destiny and misplaced trust put an end to my safe world. I was forced to survive situations I never thought I'd have to face. In doing so, I learned fear, anger, and strength are all illusions. Only Faith, love, and determination can help you come out of a bad situation the same person who went in. The wisdom gained keeps you from going back.

Christmas Presence was written at the start of my worst days. It came out of me in a rush, appearing on the pages of a yellow legal pad, the poem has stayed with me more than 25 years. Christmas Presence is dedicated to people who are lost like I was when I wrote the poem. It is also an entreaty to those who can, with a gentle word or simple act, give hope to those lost that the bad days will end.

I also dedicate this to those who stayed beside me in the dark, those who left me behind, and those who waited and prayed for me. You all taught me something. My family sacrificed much for me and never flinched at what they had to endure for my folly. My friends did the same, even some old friends I thought were out of my life.

Finally, I dedicate this to Jane who truly loved me and helped me let go of my anger.

All of you who read this have people who love you. Cherish them.

Jim

Toward the end of every year we know that Christmas Day
Will lift the tired spirits for those who celebrate
With gifts and lights and Christmas trees and carols that we sing,
And all the warm and happy smiles that Christmas presents bring.
Christmas is for everyone, but there is just one flaw
We each define our everyone and everyone's not all.
We judge what we'll be sharing by who can share with us
And sometimes even that is really not enough.
We'll make up an excuse to justify the fact
We ignore some folks we shouldn't saying, "I just can't."
For them there is no gift, nor visit, not a call,
Not even just a simple smile while rushing through the mall.
Christmas to forgotten folks becomes another day
To bear alone like all the rest that drain their lives away.
Come take a look at Christmastime for those you might have missed
When you ignored their names as you made your Christmas list.

SARA

Sara Jenkins limped along the sidewalk on South Main,
Her ancient, failing body was bent with cold and pain.
Her dirty fingers held the bags containing all she owned;
She walked alone and spoke to ghosts of people she had known.
The shoppers on the sidewalk turned away in haste,
The sight and smell of Sara was more than they could take.
No one knew old Sara, and no one wanted to;
No one had the time for her with Christmas things to do.

She hobbled down an alleyway behind *The Deli Suite*,
To find the empty packing crate where she had to sleep.
But when she turned the corner, she dropped her bags, appalled.
A big blue truck had smashed her home against the deli's wall.

Sara scrambled to the crate and pulled the boards away
Searching through the scraps of it to find a picture frame.
The glass was cracked, the photo torn, but she could see his face,
And his arm around her shoulders in a younger time and place.
Gently as she could, she pulled the picture free
And turned it to the light so that she could see.
She smiled at him and kissed him, then put him in her shirt.
She hugged herself to pull him close and wished he were with her.

The wind whipped up around her, she pulled her old coat tight.
She knew she needed someplace warm to make it through the night.
Sara spied the dumpster where she used to look for food,
The only thing the dumpster held were rags and broken wood.
She packed some rags around her, stuffed them in her clothes

And looked around to find a spot to sleep out of the snow.
There was nowhere in the alley where she could lay her head,
She had a thought, went to the truck to try the door instead.
When she braced herself and pulled, the truck door opened up,
And Sara's life grew by one night, all thanks to random luck.

The driver of the truck went home on noon for Christmas Eve,
And left something there behind him in his pell-mell haste to leave.
A thermos and a lunch box were lying on the floor;
Now Sara had a Christmas meal and shelter from the storm.

She gathered up her battered bags and slid onto the seat,
Locked the doors, settled back, and had something to eat.
If he came back in the morning, then she'd have to leave,
But time for that tomorrow, tonight was Christmas Eve.

JULIE

A painted doll in four-inch heels and dirty mini skirt
Strutted down the frigid streets, her name was Julie Kirk.
Julie looked not left nor right, she never paused at all
As she walked into the bus depot to make an urgent call.
No one seemed to notice the street girl passing by;
If they had, it's doubtful anyone would try
To talk to her or even smile, for they knew what she was.
And who would waste a moment on one who was so flawed.
Julie was a runaway who learned to play for pay,
Bad choices forced this life on her and now she'd lost her say
In how she dressed or who she saw or even when she ate;
But in her childish heart, she hoped tonight to change her fate.

In a sea of Christmas travelers, she knew she was alone;
So, she pulled herself together and grabbed the telephone.
She lifted the receiver, dialed then held it close,
But Julie couldn't speak when her mother said, "Hello?"
Tears ran out of Julie's eyes and made her makeup bleed,
Her mother's voice said softly, "Please Julie, talk to me."
Julie couldn't answer; her voice was just a choke.
Slowly she replaced the phone and killed her only hope.

She felt she'd lost the privilege of being welcomed home,
If her family should discover what she'd done out on her own.
Julie leaned her head against the hand that held the phone;
Her mother's voice had broken her, she couldn't be alone.
Even in this depot, tonight was Christmas Eve,
Someone among these people must have the eyes to see
She was just a lonely kid who wandered off the path,
Was a little Christmas kindness too much for her to ask?
Strangers' faces floated by and no one saw her face.
Julie was alone and lost inside this crowded place.

She looked around for comfort trying hard to smile.
She might have been invisible to those who passed her by.
A woman dropped a package, Julie picked it up,
Held it out with both her hands and smiled as she stood up.
The woman paused a moment, looked Julie up and down,
Then roughly took the package and left without a sound.

Her hands fell to her sides as she sat and hung her head,
Thought about the phone and what she could have said.
As everyone ignored her on this holy, silent night,
Julie sank down lower, almost out of sight.
People bustled everywhere, they were on their way
Where families were waiting for them, home on Christmas Day.

Thomas

Thomas Spence, a mailman, had walked ten thousand miles
In a small-town neighborhood where they all knew his smile.
Through rain and sleet and even snow, faithful to his oath,
Thomas brought the morning mail to all these busy folks.
At times he brought them happiness and when he saw them smile,
He'd share their joy and hang around to chat with them awhile.

When he delivered bad news, Thomas had a way
To quell their disappointment by knowing what to say.
But in the joyful moments or when the news was grim,
Or even when there was no news, no one asked of him.
Tom knew all their secrets, birthdays or who died;
He lived their lives beside them and never got inside.

At Christmastime he brought the mail to houses all decked out
With trees and colored Christmas lights and children's happy shouts.
When he delivered Christmas gifts, Thomas would pretend
The eager people watched for him because he was their friend.
When smiling faces greeted him, and each house was the same,
Thomas Spence whispered prayers, naming all their names.
He'd been thirty years among them, yet always out of reach,
They lived their lives behind closed doors where he would never be.

It's not that they forgot him, for on every Christmas Eve
They gave him socks or cookie tins and things he didn't need.
Tom was always grateful for the effort that they made
He'd laugh and smile, shake a hand, and walk off with a wave.
This Christmas, like the others, he drove away alone,
And walked into the empty house that Thomas called his home.
He placed their Christmas presents beneath his tiny tree,
And waited late to open them, alone on Christmas Eve.
He pretended they were with him and showed the gifts around,
Imagining their voices, but there wasn't any sound.

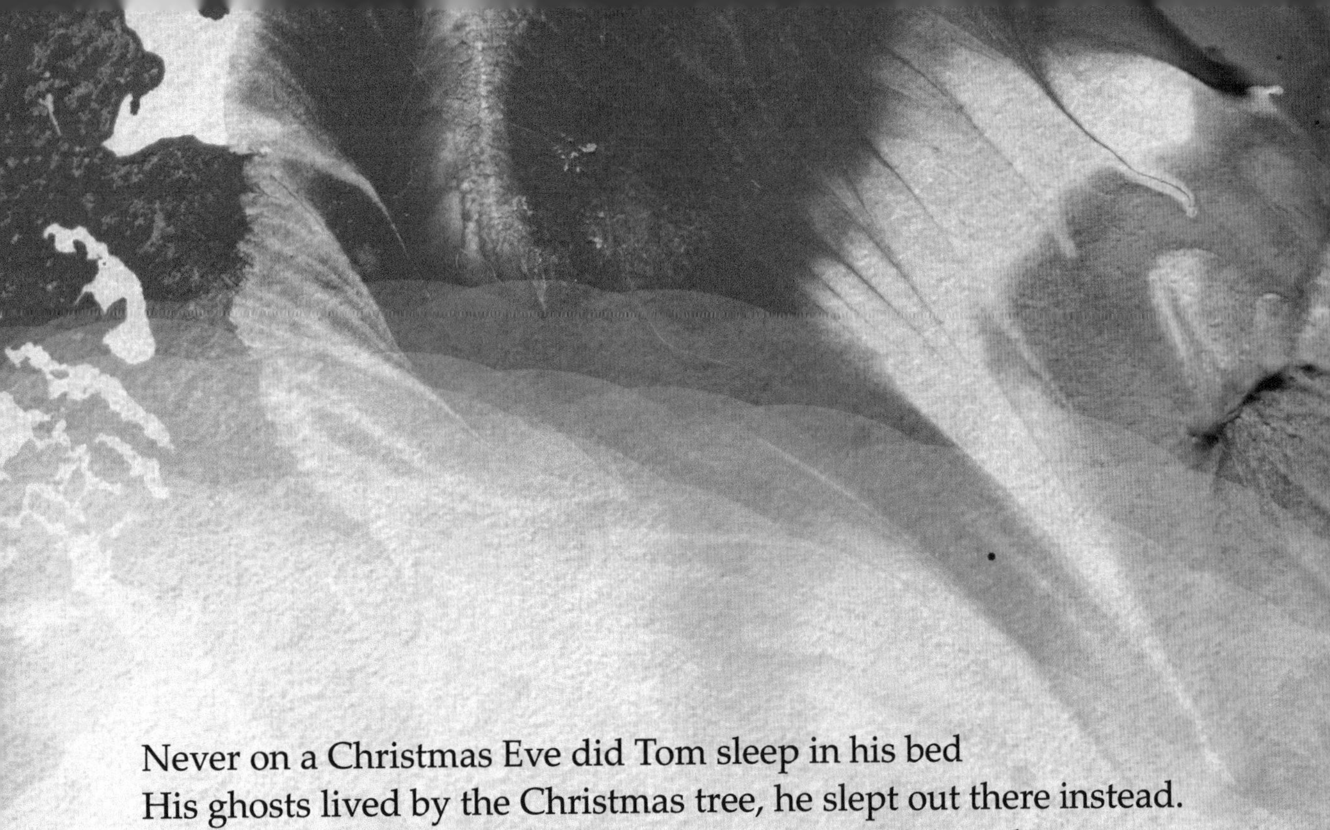

Never on a Christmas Eve did Tom sleep in his bed
His ghosts lived by the Christmas tree, he slept out there instead.
As he slept each Christmas Eve came dreams of those long gone
His wife, who dearly loved him, and his son who had moved on.
When the dreams had ended, and old Tom Spence awoke,
On Christmas Day, as always, his dreams were gone in smoke.

ANGIE

The night was falling softly sending darkness up the stairs
To the crowded rooms which Angie and her children shared
The children were alone inside, there was no lighted tree,
The only sign of Christmas was a special on TV.
Smells came from the kitchen where her daughter cooked,
The other three kept glancing at the door which they kept locked.
The apartment wasn't pretty, but the kids were clothed and fed
It took every cent she earned to keep a roof above their heads.

Footsteps on the stairway brought the children to the door
When Angie pushed it open, she stood there pale and worn.
She smiled down at her children, but what Angie couldn't say
Was she didn't have the money to give them gifts on Christmas Day.

Her husband had abandoned them and left them on their own
Without means for them to live when he found another home.
Every day since he'd been gone, she went to school or worked
The kids deserved a decent life, so Angie never shirked.
It cost her precious time from them, it cost the kids their mom,
But Angie kept her head up and always carried on.

They welcomed Angie, sat her down, and even rubbed her feet.
While Angie didn't dare to look beneath the Christmas tree
None of the children mentioned it and Angie was relieved
She got up with a weary smile and claimed that she was beat.
She told them she would nap awhile, "Please, wake me up to eat."
Then Angie went into her room and closed the door to weep.

MARIA

The Golden Harvest Nursing Home was old and cold and gray,
This was where Maria Barnes would spend her final days.
Maria was alone here, no visitors or friends.
Alone was how Maria could expect to meet her end.
Her daughter didn't want her, her son thought her a trial,
But Maria lied and told the world she'd just be here awhile:
"When Sonny's business settles down and he can take me home,
Or Peanut and her family return at last from Rome."

The truth was that Maria couldn't bear the shame
Of being dropped off in her wheelchair on the sidewalk in the rain
While Maria cried and pleaded as they drove off out of sight.
Two years ago they left her here, six hundred lonely nights.

Maria made a show of things, she always had a smile,
Never letting people know how sad she was inside.
An aide bought her some postcards; she sent them to herself
And told anyone who'd listen that they came to her from Delft,
And all the distant cities that Peanut traveled to,
But she hoped they wouldn't notice the shaky pen she used.

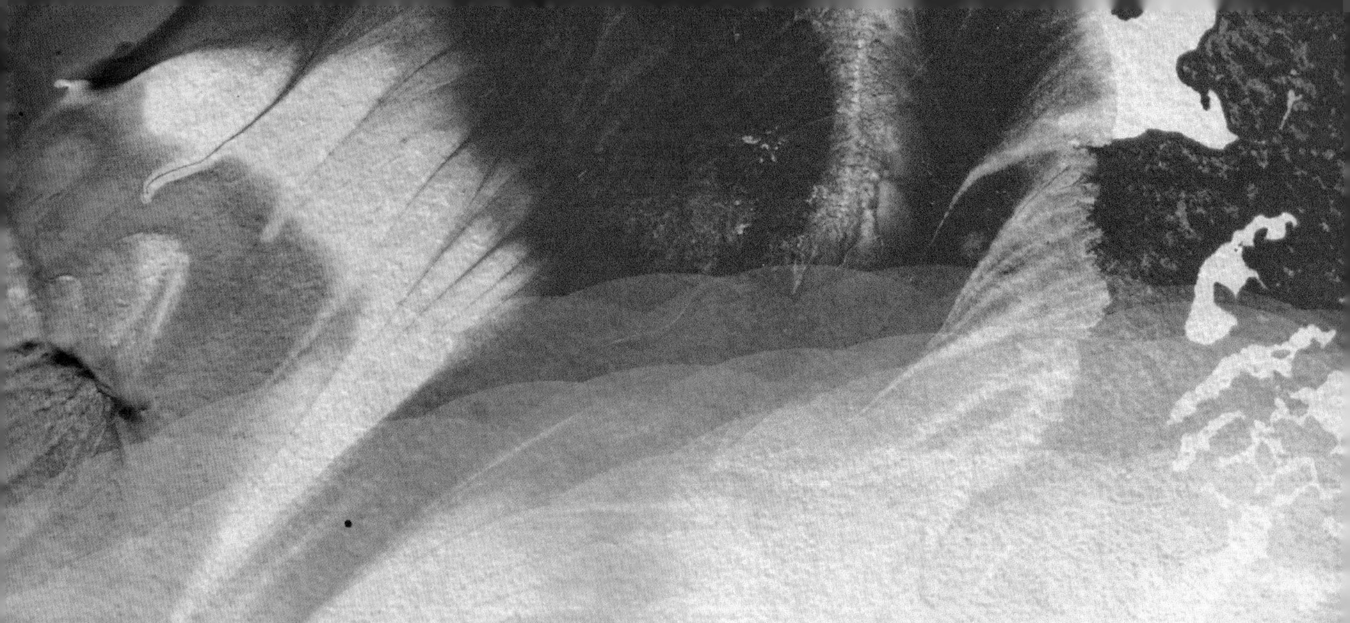

Each Christmas Eve was special; this was the time of year
Maria kept alive the hope her kids would both appear.
Just to come and see her, not to take her home.
Maria still believed they'd come because she was their mom.
It was she who changed their diapers and comforted their fears,
And when the world broke their hearts, Maria dried their tears.
She'd done it out of love for them and wanted no reward,
But a Christmas visit once a year shouldn't be so hard.

She knew she wasn't perfect, and now that she was old,
She knew she was a burden, or so she had been told
By both of them at different times. Still she had the hope
That on a Christmas sometime, she would see them both.

On Christmas Eve she dressed up, her hair had tinsel stars,
She wore a blinking reindeer on the dress above her heart.
She wheeled into the meeting room with all the other folks.
An eager smile upon her face, she wished and prayed and hoped.

Hours passed, and one by one the other families came,
But for lonely old Maria this year was just the same.
As would probably be next year and the year which followed next,
Which was two more years of Christmas than Maria could expect.

She sadly rolled the wheelchair back up to her room
And lit a Christmas candle to lighten up the gloom.
As the radio played softly the songs of Christmas Eve,
Maria sagged into her wheelchair and drifted off to sleep.

BILL

Bill Nelson was in business, a most important man,
He was always moving, he never walked, he ran.
His friends were all impressive, big shots in his town,
Who sometimes made a point to Bill that they were looking down.
He ignored the mocking tone when they called him Dollar Bill,
But Bill knew where he grew up accounted for the chill
He felt from all his buddies when he turned his back.
Because Dollar Bill, their rich friend, grew up across the tracks.
Though Dollar Bill tried everything he never could fit in;
And for each success he had, his friends resented him.
His wife he'd known from high school, a lovely tender girl,
Had no use at all for her husband's fast paced world.
His life cost more than dollars, she knew he couldn't see
That one day soon, if he kept on, he'd lose his family.
His wife had always loved him and made their place a home,
She still had hope he loved her, though she felt all alone.
He had another woman and thought his wife was blind
Fun was all he wanted when his girl stole family time.
He ran through all his days and snuck through all his nights
And never saw the burning bridges that he left behind.
The children didn't know him, although they loved him too,
And explained away his absence with, "Dad has work to do."

Every Christmas Eve, Nelson's wife made family plans
To keep them all together, but she'd never had a chance.
At night he had his meetings, his business took the days.
He lied up lame excuses in a dozen different ways,
To keep himself away from home and striving for a goal,
That all his mindless striving had cost him long ago.

But this year would be different, this year she would win,
She made a plan to get Bill home for dinner with the kids.
The store would close at noon that day. She made him promise her
To run some Christmas errands. Bill gave his solemn word
He'd be on time for dinner with all the errands run
He told her she could count on him and she thought she had won.

The kids got more excited as the dinnertime got near,
A Christmas Eve together, the first they'd spend in years!
At five o'clock his first call came, at six o'clock they ate.
At eight o'clock still no Bill, at ten o'clock he came.

His shirt had stains of lipstick; his suit coat smelled of smoke.
His arms were filled with presents; he slurred the words he spoke.
"Well, you guys, old daddy's home, let's have our Christmas Eve!"
By 10:15, out on the couch, Bill Nelson was asleep.

THE MIRACLES

Christmas Presence isn't wrapped and placed beneath our trees
The Presence that is Christmas lives in you and me.
We can give this Presence freely, it only costs us time
And the happiness it brings, lasts beyond the giver's life
In ripples that flow outward for lives and lives to come
Of those who learn to share it because it blessed them once.
Some suffer through their Christmas though not from lack of gifts.
They suffer from the empty feeling caused by loneliness.

This painful sorrow has a cure, a simple loving thing,
Come, look again and see the joy that spending time can bring:

The driver of the truck that crushed old Sara's hut
On Christmas Day remembered he hadn't it locked it up.
He went down to the alley and found her sleeping there
And the thought of this poor woman in the cold he couldn't bear.
The driver gently woke her, at first, she was afraid
When he said, "Merry Christmas, Ma," she felt her fears allayed.
He said, "The family's waiting and we have an extra place.
What say you come home with me and share our Christmas Day?"
Sara searched his smiling face afraid this was a ruse
And saw a soft reflection of another face she knew.
For the first time in a decade this wandering soul would know
What it felt to share a Christmas with a family in their home

Julie Kirk, the runaway, so lost and all alone
Looked up into a stranger's smile, he'd seen her on the phone.
She feared he was her next one and prepared herself for that
He nodded as he said hello, then smiled at her, and sat.
He spoke to her so softly not of the things she feared;
She found his words transported her far away from here.
He said that she reminded him of the daughter that he loved.
He had his daughter's picture – she was giving him a hug.
He replaced it in his pocket with sadness in his eyes
"What I'd give for one more hug…last Christmas Eve, she died."
The wall broke down in Julie; she sobbed and hugged him close
Twenty minutes later he bought her ticket home.
He sat there and encouraged her until the right bus came
He put her on, and waved good-bye. She never knew his name.

Tom Spence woke alone again beside the Christmas tree
And felt the loss of magic from the dreams of Christmas Eve.
He lay upon the couch, his forearm on his head
And searched the ceiling for a clue of why this was his stead.
As he lay there thinking, Tom's front doorbell rang
And he thought it was left over from the pleasant dreams he had.
He closed his eyes to visualize, again the doorbell rang,
So Tom got up and opened it as thirty people sang
Christmas carols for the friend who brought them more than mail.
There was one of them for every year he shared his friendly smile.
By the time that they had finished, Tom felt warm and young
With all his lonely holidays erased by just this one.

Angie joined the children smiling, said she couldn't sleep.
And she made herself look happy when they sat down to eat.
She praised the special dinner and said that she was stuffed
Before she really was so the kids would have enough.
Later, with them all in bed she sat down in a chair
And felt the tears start up again - then she saw a letter there
It simply said: "To Angie," had her address and a stamp.
Fifteen seconds later there was money in her hand.
Five hundred-dollar bills were in a simple penciled note
That wished her Merry Christmas and a joyous New Year hope.

The tears leaked out, she turned to see the clock up on the wall;
Whoever sent this gift left time for Christmas after all!
Some stores would still be open so she could buy them gifts
And have some cash left over to pass tomorrow's shift.
There would be enough for this year, so here's what Angie did.

Maria was awakened by an aide on Christmas morn,
She said, "Get up, come with me while breakfast is still warm."
Maria tried to stay in bed; the aide had none of it.
"Come on, you Grinch, it's Christmas, Santa brought you gifts."
Maria climbed into her chair; she was sadly calm.
When they got down to the great room, she heard a man say, "Mom."
Maria raised her head and saw them by the tree;
Her son, his wife, the grandkids, who ran to her in glee.
She hugged them to her fiercely, their mother stroked her hair.
Her daughter-in-law was smiling through eyes that truly cared.
Her son knelt down beside her, "Mom," the man began,
"Please, will you come home with us?" Bill Nelson took her hand.

These aren't simply stories; they're choices that we make
To take some time that's given us and give the gift away.
Not just every Christmas, but every day of life,
The greatest presents we can give are gifts of precious time.

ABOUT THE AUTHOR

Christmas Presence is the first work Jim Timonere published. It was written more than 25 years ago in a jail cell where Jim had been confined after a bitterly fought trial that saw him convicted of drug charges he still denies. Prior to being convicted, Jim had been a lawyer, politician, and a family man. After almost seven years of incarceration, he was alone, had lost his license to practice law and was forced to rebuild his life from nothing. Christmas Presence has travelled with Jim through all of this. Those who read it over the years find Christmas Presence moving to the point that some families read it aloud every year on Christmas Eve.

Jim has also written a short novel, The Present from Christmas Past, which is available on Amazon Books and Kindle.

Jim now lives with his wife, Jane, in his hometown of Ashtabula, Ohio. Jim works as a paralegal in Jane's law practice. Between them, Jim and Jane have six children and ten grandchildren. The Timonere's like to travel when they can take time away from Jane's practice. They hope one day to retire to Lake Tahoe.

Printed in Great
Britain
by Amazon